BIBLE BRIDES:
Trials and Triumphs

BEVERLY ROBERTSON

WESTBOW
PRESS®
A DIVISION OF THOMAS NELSON
& ZONDERVAN

This is a work of fiction. All of the characters, names, incidents, organizations, and dialogue in this novel are either the products of the author's imagination or are used fictitiously.

WestBow Press books may be ordered through booksellers or by contacting:

WestBow Press
A Division of Thomas Nelson & Zondervan
1663 Liberty Drive
Bloomington, IN 47403
www.westbowpress.com
1 (866) 928-1240

Because of the dynamic nature of the Internet, any web addresses or links contained in this book may have changed since publication and may no longer be valid. The views expressed in this work are solely those of the author and do not necessarily reflect the views of the publisher, and the publisher hereby disclaims any responsibility for them.

Any people depicted in stock imagery provided by Thinkstock are models, and such images are being used for illustrative purposes only.
Certain stock imagery © Thinkstock.

ISBN: 978-1-9736-0972-8 (sc)
ISBN: 978-1-9736-0973-5 (hc)
ISBN: 978-1-9736-0971-1 (e)

Library of Congress Control Number: 2017918644

Print information available on the last page.

WestBow Press rev. date: 1/4/2018

DEDICATION

These stories were written for my granddaughters and grand nieces. I wanted to acquaint them with these amazing Biblical women. So I dedicate this book to:

Granddaughters:

Kaitlyn Robertson
Elizabeth Kallay
Kathrine Kallay
Zoey Gibbs
Leita Yott

All My Grand Nieces

Contents

ACKNOWLEDGMENTS

Special thanks to family and friends who listened to my stories and helped with the photographs in this book.

Thanks to my editor, Amy Harke-Moore, who kept me on track while correcting my errors.

I raise my cup to my writing friend Pat Reiter, who shared critiques and encouragement over many steaming refills of coffee.

My thanks to my parents, who nurtured and encouraged me in the Christian faith.

Many hugs to my husband for putting up with my midnight trips to my computer to click in some stray thoughts.

Introduction

Have you ever wondered what it was like to be a bride in biblical times? If you have, you may have thought about how different the culture was then and how few choices the women had in determining their own destiny. However, this is a collection of seven stories about eight strong women who, in spite of their social limitations, triumphed in their own rights over difficult circumstances.

These biblical women had to sometimes overcome the heartbreak of being one of multiple wives and having fathers who determined whom they would marry. Some fathers were more interested in the dowry they could receive by marrying off a beautiful and intelligent daughter. Some faced life-threatening decisions and were selfless in caring for others. Thus, these are some of the problems our heroines faced.

Yes, you will be reading about a very different time period, but you also will find out these were girls with the same thoughts and feelings you may have, and the same spirit of loyalty, caring, and love of romance. You will admire their courage and spunk in coping with the circumstances they have been dealt and sometimes overriding what their culture expects from them.

I hope you will discover that there was romance in the Bible and that though time and cultures have thankfully changed, these were real people like us. I hope this will spark your interest in this amazing book we call the Bible. Here you will find many more stories and truths and a guide to live by. In the New Testament, Jesus promises to help us with any problem we may have so that we may triumph as well.

CHAPTER 1

A Prayer for a Bride

REBEKAH HOISTED THE LARGE WATER jug on her shoulder and began walking toward the well. The sun was low in the sky, bringing relief from the heat of the day. She looked forward to the coolness of the subterranean, spring-fed well and the chance to talk to the other young women. Sometimes travelers from distant places passed by, and she would wonder what life was like beyond her horizon.

As she walked, her mind was troubled by what she had overheard her older brother, Laban, say to one of her other brothers the night before. "We need to find a husband for Rebekah soon. She is almost too old to marry, and our family will be disgraced." Then he named several possible contenders, each one quite wealthy but far too old and disgusting.

Obviously Laban was only thinking of the marriage dowry, not of her happiness. He was in charge of her marriage arrangements, and she feared who he might choose.

Rebekah's brisk pace slowed as she spotted an unusual sight. Ten camels with caretakers and drivers surrounded the well. An elderly, well-clothed man was bent over praying. She couldn't hear his words but watched as he earnestly put forth his petitions to a God he sincerely believed in.

She drew her water and was about to leave when the man spoke to her. "Young woman, would you be kind enough to give me a drink?"

"Certainly," she replied, as this was common courtesy. Then she heard herself say, "I'll water your camels too." What was she thinking by offering to tend to ten camels, including all of the trips it would take to fill their trough? She would have to descend the stone stairs circling deep into the ground, fill her heavy clay jug, and climb back up.

Still, she kept her word, and as she worked, the old man bowed his head and prayed again. She heard him mention something about the God of Abraham sending an angel to help him find his master's family.

When she had finished, she counted about eighty trips and wiped her brow, which was covered in perspiration.

The old man looked up and asked, "Whose daughter are you?"

"My father is Bethuel, son of Nahor," she replied.

"Would he have room for us tonight?"

She nodded graciously. "Yes, we have plenty of room at home for you and your camels."

"Thank you for your kindness. My name is Eliezar, the servant of your relative Abraham." He presented her with a gold nose ring with an exquisite, dainty heart pendant.

Rebekah was awed by his gift. All the other girls at the well had left by now, but she couldn't wait to show them and to see her reflection. That evening, she would put the ring in her right nostril, which was the way all of the women wore them. She picked up her jug to leave.

"Wait," Eliezar called out.

Rebekah turned around.

"My master sent these for you too," he said.

She watched in disbelief when he told her to hold out her hands. In them, he dropped two beautifully crafted gold bracelets.

"Sir, are you sure?" Rebekah wondered if the man was too old to know what he was doing.

He gave her a vigorous nod. "I know he'd want you to have them."

Rebekah decided to accept her good fortune and hurried home to tell everyone.

She told her family, "Come! We have to prepare for a guest who has ten camels to feed and bed down!"

"Are you in your right mind?" Laban objected. "We don't have the time to bother with a traveler—and least of all his dirty beasts."

"Think again, brother," Rebekah warned. "Look at the two gold bracelets and ring he gave me. Besides, the traveler is the servant of Abraham."

The gold jewelry particularly impressed Laban when she held out her arm for him to inspect. He ran his fingers over one of the bracelets and raised his eyebrows. "These are worth about ten shekels and would take a long time to earn." He turned his head sideways. "You're right. I see that we do have reason to treat them properly."

That evening as the men gathered for their meal, Rebekah and her mother convinced the maid, Deborah, to listen and tell them what the men talked about.

When Deborah returned, she said, "Rebekah, didn't you know you were being prayed about and tested at the well?"

"No. Tell us more," Rebekah replied.

"The old man you met is the servant of Abraham, who is the brother of Nahor. He was traveling to look for a bride for his master's son. He prayed that God's angel would guide him to the right girl. As a sign, she would give him a drink and water all his camels."

Rebekah's eyes widened as she put her hand to her heart. "Why, that is just what I did!" she exclaimed. "Does he think that I'm the one he's looking for?"

"Yes. He said so to Laban. I even heard your brother whisper to your other brothers that this would mean more dowry than he had expected. Later the man brought out jewels, expensive rugs, and garments for you and every family member."

Rebekah's heart beat faster as she listened. "This is my chance at a new life—maybe with a man nearer my age—and to venture beyond my homeland."

"Oh, Rebekah, are you sure you want to go? You'll be so far away, and we'll never see you again," her mother moaned.

"Dear Mother, I will surely miss you too, but if I don't go with them, Laban will marry me off to someone of his choosing, not mine. Besides, if my meeting Eliezar by the well was the will of God, I believe it will be for the best."

The next morning at daybreak, Rebekah was called to meet at once with her family. She found her mother and older brothers waiting outside her mother's tent.

Laban spoke. "We've decided that you are to marry Isaac, the son of Abraham," he said. "However, we know how difficult you can be and ask if you're willing to go on this long journey."

She nodded and murmured, "Yes."

"But his servant cannot wait ten days before leaving, as your mother requested. He must return to Abraham at once."

Rebekah's eyes met her mother's as she responded, "So be it. I believe it's God's will. Yes, I will go."

Her family gave their approval. "Let us pronounce our blessing upon you."

Rebekah knelt before them, and they said these words over her: "Our sister, may you become the mother of many millions! May your descendants overcome all your enemies."

Then Laban said, "Now you must take Deborah, your childhood nurse, choose your maidens, and gather your things. You are to be ready to leave before sunrise."

Rebekah did as she was told, with excitement welling up in her heart as she tried to envision her bridegroom. Still she warned herself not to become too hopeful but to trust in God's continued guidance.

The trip proved to be long and hard, lasting about a month. They traveled through mountains, deserts, and plains, but she enjoyed seeing all these sights and found the people in the villages intriguing. During this time, her curiosity got the best of her. She couldn't help but ask her camel driver, "What's he like?"

"He's somewhat older than you, about forty, but don't worry. He's strong and handsome."

As they progressed farther, the land flourished with grain, a welcome change from the monotonous stretches of sand and merciless sun. Soon the servant told her they were approaching his master's home, and she was to prepare to meet her groom.

Rebekah spotted a young man walking through the field toward the caravan. As he drew closer, she could see he was muscular, with dark, wavy hair and a beard. He walked with a confident air, and his robe was of fine fabric befitting a landowner of means. He was more handsome than she had ever dreamed. She hoped with all her heart this was Isaac.

She called for her camel driver to stop. Then she slid down from her perch and asked, "Pray tell me who this young man is."

"Mistress, this is Isaac, the one you have traveled so far to meet."

Rebekah quickly covered her face with a large, long veil and wrapped it around her, for it was customary for a bride to be covered in the presence of her groom until the wedding. She could see Isaac talking to Eliezar and knew he was giving him a brief summary of all that had taken place. Then his gaze met hers, and all the dust, hot sand, and camel stench melted away into oblivion. He stretched out his hand for her, and she was delighted to accept it as they walked on to the encampment together. She could tell by the look in his eyes he was pleased with her. She was determined to convince him she was worthy of all that had been done on her behalf.

Isaac spoke to her as they walked. "We have long awaited your arrival and are happy to see everyone has endured the journey. Much preparation has been made for you and your maidens. They will be shown to their tents and given what they need."

As they strolled past several wells, a sign of the family's wealth, he continued speaking. "These were dug by my father and provide us with plenty of water." Then his gaze went to the hills, where animals grazed. "My father and I have been blessed with many herds. And here is my late mother's tent. She has been gone for three years. But now it's yours."

Rebekah could hear the sadness in his voice and vowed she'd make him happy.

"If you would like," he said, "you may rest for a while and get ready for tonight's feast."

As she stepped inside, she was in awe of the beautiful tapestry, carpets, golden urns, and basins. Before Isaac left her, he told her that someone would come for her when it was time. "I want you to meet my father, Abraham. He will pray a blessing over us if this meets with your approval."

He looked into her eyes as he spoke with such kindness

and charm that she just nodded her head and said softly, "I'd be honored."

After he left, Rebecca thought, *He is so handsome, caring––the man I've always dreamed of. I'm glad I've trusted this God.*

A servant ushered her to the elaborate feast with some unfamiliar but delicious food. She met Abraham and reverently listened to his blessing he pronounced on their marriage. Now Isaac walked beside her to her tent. Rebekah noticed genuine respect from the servants, who bowed as they passed. She had never experienced a night this beautiful with the heavens so full of stars. Her heart danced as she realized the man beside her was the brightest star of all. She gradually unwrapped her long veil, and as it slipped from her face, Isaac exclaimed. "How very beautiful you are! You have been worth waiting for."

How fortunate she was to have found a husband as wonderful as Isaac!

Thus Rebekah and Isaac began married life and sought to have a family. After about twenty years, they had fraternal twins, Esau and Jacob. Through these sons, Rebekah eventually fulfilled her family's blessing of becoming the mother of millions.

This story is found in Genesis 24.

CHAPTER 2

Betrayal of Two Brides

RACHEL LIFTED THE FLAP OF her tent as the glorious hues of dawn cast their brilliance on the hills of Haran. Her flock of sheep bleated, restless to leave their pen for the open pastures. She was in her early teens, and she loved being a shepherdess and had earned the respect of the male herders. Her name was befitting, as it meant *ewe*. However, she had one daily nagging thought––who would her greedy father marry her off to, and would he be someone old and dreadful?

"Before you go, I'll give you a piece of this warm bread,"

Leah, Rachel's older sister, said. Leah's large-boned body turned as she slid the brown, crusty bread out from the stone oven and approached Rachel with eyes that were too big for her face. It was those eyes that might have led to her name, meaning *wild cow*.

"Thanks, your breads are so good," Rachel muttered as she left to get the sheep. She was glad to escape the cooking and domestic chores that Leah was so good at.

When the sun was high in the sky, she took her herd to the well. Some of the shepherds were already there, and she stopped for a moment when she saw a foreigner chatting among them.

"Here comes Laban's daughter now," one of them said.

"She's so lovely," the stranger said as his smiling eyes followed her. When she came closer, he bowed. "Please let me remove the stone, and I'll water your sheep."

Rachel greeted his offer with a nod and sat down on the hillside in the waving grass and wrapped her arms around her knees. She observed his intelligent eyes set in a handsome face and watched his muscles ripple when he lifted the earthen jars.

After he finished the task, Rachel stood. "Thank you for your kindness. Why would you, a stranger, be so helpful?"

"My name is Jacob, and I'm a relative. I have traveled a long way." He impulsively bent over and kissed her and sighed with relief that his difficult journey was over.

She could feel her stomach fluttering, but Rachel quickly came to her senses and confronted his behavior with a stern, questioning look.

Jacob held up the palms of his hands. "It's the custom to greet family. Your father is the brother of my mother, Rebekah, and she said he would give me lodging."

"Watch the flock, and I'll run ahead and tell him you're here," Rachel said.

Rachel was breathless when she arrived at Laban's tent. "Father, Jacob, Rebekah's son, has just arrived and wants to meet you."

So Laban went out to greet Jacob. "Welcome. Come back with me and stay as long as you wish. Seeing you reminds me of your mother and how your father blessed us with so many gifts."

Rachel found Leah stirring a pot of stew over an open fire. "Leah, I've just met the most incredible man, and he's our kinsman from Canaan."

Leah looked at Rachel as she tapped her spoon on the rim of the caldron, and the savory juices dripped back into the mixture. Leah's interest began to rise to a simmer as she placed one hand on her hip and waved the utensil toward Rachel. "Tell me more."

"He helped me water all the sheep, and … he kissed me!" Rachel said.

Now Leah's interest rose to a boil. It was hard having such

a beautiful sister while she was so unattractive. Although Leah knew she had superb domestic skills, being in her late teens, she felt the sting of no prospects for marriage.

"You always get so carried away. I'll judge for myself when I see him," Leah said.

That evening as Jacob walked by to enter their father's tent, Rachel whispered, "See, what did I tell you?"

Leah gazed at the stranger. "You were right. He is mysterious and so handsome."

They stood nearby, pretending to take care of the food, and strained to hear the conversation between Laban and Jacob.

"What brings you so far away from your home? Surely your father has prospered and your family is well." Laban asked. "Were you robbed on the way?"

"Everyone is fine, but I received my father's blessing before my older twin, Esau. He claimed I had tricked him, and I had to flee for my life with only survival supplies," Jacob said. "But I managed my father's herds and am willing to help you."

After a month, Laban again summoned Jacob to share a meal with him. Rachel and Leah found an excuse to be nearby.

"I've come to realize your management skills are excellent, and everything you do has flourished," their father said. "Jacob, how can I pay you?"

"As you know, I have nothing to give you for a dowry, but if you will give me Rachel for my wife, I will work for you for seven years."

Laban said, "That's a generous offer. I would rather give her to you than someone not in the family."

"You won't regret it," Jacob said.

Rachel was elated when she heard of her betrothal to Jacob but caught a glimpse of Leah's downcast face as she turned to gather the serving pots.

"I might have known you would marry before me. Either no one has asked Father or he expects too large a dowry," Leah said.

"He probably hates to lose you. You bake the breads to perfection and flavor the meats with exotic spices purchased from caravans." Rachel's eyes met Leah's.

When the men departed, Rachel and Leah observed the smile on Jacob's face—and the smirk on Laban's lips.

In the following days when Rachel walked to the well, she could see Jacob's eyes light up every time she came near. She looked forward to their brief times together. He told her of his life in Canaan and how God had appeared to him in a dream and promised him many descendants. Then he would ask her to play her flute.

"I love to hear your music. How did you learn to play like that?" Jacob asked with an admiring look.

"An old shepherd taught me when he showed me how

to care for the sheep. I try to capture the sound of the wind blowing through the trees or the chirping of the birds," Rachel said.

Meanwhile Leah also found Jacob irresistible. One evening as Jacob passed Leah preparing the meal, he surprised her by discussing the various seasonings his mother had used. She savored his shared confidence, but she knew he had eyes only for Rachel.

One day as Leah entered Laban's tent to shake out the rugs, her father remarked, "Leah, Jacob's seven years are up, and it's time for us to prepare for the wedding." Her arms stretched in midair, froze, and then dropped the rug. She turned to leave as Laban caught her wrist. "Why, Leah, you love him too. Don't you?"

While Leah was making her hasty retreat, her father said, "Leah, I want to talk to you after the evening meal, and make sure you're alone."

Days later, strains of music and sounds of laughter floated among the tents of Laban. The silhouettes of men eating and drinking too much stood out against the moonlight. Rachel sat dressed in her wedding robe, wearing her veil and waiting hours for her father to come get her. Finally she fell asleep, resting her head on her arms.

Jacob became impatient and demanded, "Laban, why are you stalling? Bring me my bride."

At last Laban did as Jacob requested.

As the rays of the morning light peeked into the nuptial tent, Jacob's eyes fluttered open to gaze upon his beloved and then opened wide. This was the moment Leah dreaded. She had been ushered into the bridal tent heavily veiled and under the cover of darkness, instructed by her father not to say a word. She agreed to the plan because she thought this was her only chance to get a good husband. Her father was a polygamist and convinced her Jacob would love her too, but one look at his horrified face erased all hope. She watched as he threw on his robe to confront her father.

Jacob grabbed the snoring Laban from his mat, bringing him to his feet. "Why have you tricked me after the seven years I worked for Rachel?"

Laban, now wide awake, replied, "It's our custom to marry the oldest daughter first. Leah will make a good wife."

"I only wanted one wife—Rachel," Jacob shouted loud enough to be heard throughout the encampment.

"All right, Jacob. I'll tell you what I'll do. After the bridal week, you can have Rachel also if you will work another seven years."

Jacob stared in disbelief. "You snake. I can't believe this after all my faithful years of service!"

Laban leered at Jacob. "I believe you love her enough to do it."

"All right, Laban," Jacob answered, "but I'll never trust you again."

Upon leaving, Jacob whirled around and flipped the two tent poles as they went spinning to the ground, and the tent of goat skins flopped upon Laban and left him looking like a lumpy statue.

In the meantime, Rachel awoke to Jacob's raging bellows. She shook her head, surprised she was still in her own tent. Realizing what had happened, she dissolved into tears. She threw off her wedding attire, put on the closest robe, and headed out to face her father. "How could you?"

Still weeping, Rachel saw a look of dismay on Laban's face. Perhaps he realized what he had done as the sobs of Leah resonated from her tent, knowing she was still unloved. Then she turned to look at the misery in Jacob's face.

Leah asked for Rachel to come so she could speak with her. "I'm sorry," Leah said. "I realize Jacob only loves you, and he will marry you also at the end of the week. Our father told me I had three choices. The first was to never have a husband, wed old Nabor and become his fifth wife, or marry Jacob. When I protested, he said Jacob would love me too, and I had better obey him or he'd disown me."

Rachel gasped. "Our father has wronged all of us." Then she turned on her heel and started running. She ran until she collapsed, exhausted, on a grassy knoll. She stayed there until her eyes became dry.

At last, the week was up. There was no celebration, but Jacob and Rachel would be together. Jacob took her hand, kissed her, and pulled her close. "Rachel, although Leah is my wife also, you are first in my heart."

Laban gave each bride a maid for a wedding gift. Leah's maid was Zilpah, and Rachel's was Bilhah.

Time passed, and Leah and Rachel grew accustomed to married life. Within a matter of years, Leah gave birth to four sons. Often the sisters did their chores together, with Leah stopping every now and then to settle little tiffs between her young sons.

"Maybe Jacob doesn't love me like I wish he did," she said one day as she wrung out her wash, "but I know God does because He gave me these children, all sons." Leah then laid little robes out to dry in the sun.

Leah's words stung Rachel to her core. *Why doesn't God love me too?* She had to stand by and watch Leah give birth to four sons while she remained barren.

"I have a plan to obtain a child," Rachel mumbled to herself.

Overhearing, Leah asked, "What might that be?"

"Never mind. I've got some thinking to do." Desperate, Rachel mulled the idea over in her mind. *As much as it pains me, I need a surrogate to have children. Ahh, Bilhah is the most likely person to do this.*

So, as was customary, Bilhah had two sons, which Rachel loved as her own. Leah became jealous and wanted more children. Her maid, Zilpah, had two more sons for Leah to raise. Rachel continued to turn to God, pleading to have her own child, until He heard her. Eventually, Rachel had a son named Joseph.

One day Jacob called his wives together to confer with them. Rachel sat with Leah, wondering what Jacob was about to say. She could tell it was something important as he seemed nervous, rubbing his beard and blinking his eyes.

"These past six years, your father has tried to keep my herds small by giving me the striped and spotted animals in payment. In spite of this, God has increased them until the grazing grounds have become crowded. Relations between your father and brothers and me are becoming strained."

"Our father has not changed much. He's still trying to cheat us," Rachel added and looked over at Leah, who was nodding in agreement.

Jacob folded his arms, and a serious frown crossed his face. "I'm asking you a very important question. Are you both willing to leave your homeland and go away with me?"

"Yes," they unanimously replied.

But before they left, Rachel took Laban's idols. Maybe

she did it for revenge, but Laban chased after them, and Rachel successfully hid them. Nevertheless, Jacob pronounced a curse of death on anyone who had them, not knowing it was Rachel.

On their way to Canaan, tragedy struck. Leah sat outside her tent, heartbroken, and watched Jacob racked with grief as he stood over a grave. Rachel died giving birth to her second son, Benjamin. But Leah couldn't give in to her sorrow for long. She had a fragile newborn and Joseph to care for besides her own older children.

Now Jacob came to only one tent—Leah's. After the children were asleep, the two sat by the fire and watched the sparks spiral into the starlit sky. Jacob put his arms around Leah, and she leaned into him.

"The flames remind me of Rachel and how she would laugh, dance, and play her flute," Jacob said.

"Even when we were little girls, her laughter was contagious." As the fire cast its flickering light on Leah's face, she continued. "I can still see her caring for a lamb or an injured sheep."

Jacob reached for Leah's hand. "Yes, she had a way with animals. I miss hearing her serenade them with her haunting melodies."

"We'll always be able to hear her in our minds and hearts," Leah said.

Although Rachel was her rival, Leah wished with all

her being she was still there. Jacob and Leah sat in each other's embrace with their tears mingled together until the embers grew dim. They drew strength from each other to face the daily tasks of caring for their family.

When they arrived in Canaan, Jacob brought gifts to his brother, Esau, and restored the relationship. Rachel's son Joseph eventually rose to power in Egypt and saved his family from a famine. Through her son Judah, Leah was in the lineage of Christ.

God used these imperfect people to form a nation because they allowed Him to work through them. Thus, this family of twelve sons became the twelve tribes of Israel.

This story is found in Genesis 29:1–30.

CHAPTER 3

Window of Salvation

RAHAB PULLED BACK HER LONG, dark hair as she walked over to her window to view the sunrise. Her dwelling was high on the wall of the city of Jericho and allowed her to see the expanse of fertile fields reaching west of the Jordan River, which often overflowed. She leaned forward to get a better look. Suddenly, she couldn't believe her eyes. This morning the river had vanished! The strange sight sent a cold chill through her. All that was left of the mighty Jordan was a dry riverbed with four men carrying an ornate chest on poles. Behind them a crowd of people waited on the far side, ready to charge across.

It's happening, she thought. *The Israelis are coming to destroy our city. Their powerful God has even dried up the river for them.* She was sure Jericho would not stand a chance even though the people put their trust in its thick walls.

Rahab's thoughts raced back to a few weeks ago when two men knocked on her door. One man kept looking behind him with furtive glances. His sly attitude didn't surprise her. Rahab was painfully aware she was just a harlot who ran an inn. Somehow, though, these men were different. She guessed they were Israelites who served the real God, whom she knew was the Lord God, "the God in heaven above and on earth beneath." He had helped the Israelites cross the Red Sea and be victorious in their conquests. She had long ago lost faith in lesser gods like Baal and Moloch, who demanded infant sacrifices and did not save her when the king and his men captured her. As beautiful as she was, her family was not prominent enough for her to become his bride. Fortunately, she had convinced the king to give her a house even though she realized that doomed her to the life of a harlot who would never have the respect of marriage. Her family tolerated her because she was generous with her hard-earned income. How she longed to be loved for herself.

When the two men reached her doorstep, they spoke excitedly. "Hurry, we are being followed," they warned.

At that moment, Rahab made a life-changing decision. "Come in quickly," she heard herself say. "Follow me up the ladder and to the rooftop, where I can hide you."

One of the men was young and handsome. He eyed her suspiciously. "How do we know you won't betray us?"

"You don't have a choice," she said as she led them up to the roof. She made them hide inside a large basket, which she covered with long, soggy, stinking flax stalks.

That evening, there was fierce pounding on Rahab's door. She crouched in fear as she heard a voice shouting, "Let us in or we'll break down the door!"

It must be the king's guards, she thought. As soon as she had collected herself, she let them in.

"How may I help you?" she asked, willing herself to look calm and unafraid.

"We believe two spies from the camps of Israel have come this way, and we suspect they are here," one burly guard said.

"Yes, two men were here," she admitted. "I didn't know they were spies, but they left through the city gates before nightfall and headed for the river. If you hurry, perhaps you can catch them."

As soon as the king's men were gone and she felt safe,

Rahab went to the roof and motioned for the two to follow her to her window.

"I know who you are and will try to help you, but before I get my rope to let you down over the wall, you must promise that when you come back to take the city, you will save me and my family. The hearts of the people of the city melt from fear of your God and the exploits of your army."

The older man assured her quickly, "Your mercy this day will not be forgotten as our God has indeed promised us this land, and we will be victorious. We swear by the Lord God of Israel, we will do as you ask. However, as a sign when our soldiers come, you must leave a scarlet cord hanging from this window so they will know which house is to be spared."

The handsome younger man introduced himself as Solman. Rahab handed him the scarlet rope she had made so he could hang it to the metal rung in the middle of the window.

"You can trust us," he said.

There was something about the way he looked at her that reassured Rahab. She confided in him about the king's guards searching for spies. "I told them you headed to the river, so it would be good for you to hide in the hills for a while before crossing back to your people."

Rahab had not told any of her family for fear of a slip up that would threaten her life as well as theirs. She hurried to her parents' home, exclaiming, "The Israelites are coming to take our city! You must come to my place to be safe. I've made an agreement with them to spare my house and everyone in it from destruction."

"What are you talking about?" her father demanded. "Your house on the wall is the most dangerous place. Nevertheless, the walls will keep us safe. Our ancestors helped lay the stones. How can these Israelites penetrate a wall as tall as six men standing on top of each other and wider than two men lying sideways? No enemy can destroy it." He put his hand on his chin. "I remember when the Israelites wanted to take our city many years ago and gave up."

"The walls of Jericho won't hold up against their God. Come look for yourself and see that the River Jordan is dried up and the Israelis are crossing as I speak."

When her father looked out and saw the dry river bed, his face was ashen. "You're right! We must hurry and get all of the family here."

They convinced their kin to come to her place of refuge and were careful not to arouse any suspicion. The family gathered in her home and watched from the window as the Israelites now camped on their side of the river. After their feet touched dry land, they built an altar from the stones that were exposed from the rolled-back waters. Then the river came rushing back and flowing as hard as before.

Later Rahab told her family, "I'm glad you believed me as they are now circling our city. They have been silently doing this once every six days except for the blowing of their trumpets."

The next morning was the seventh day and the Israelis marched around not only once, but six times. Then on the seventh trip, they blew the trumpets in unison and shouted with many voices. In one instant Rahab heard the crunching, cracking, and groaning of the city walls as they came crashing down.

She climbed over debris to her window, which was now partially jutting against the azure sky like some ancient ruin. The scarlet cord still swayed among decimation and dust. Scanning the scene below, Rahab recognized the two men at the head of the advancing army.

"They're coming! Get ready to go," she told her family. "The younger and stronger, help the elderly and children run for safety."

The two former spies burst into the room. "Gather your family and follow us before the rest of the soldiers get here," they warned.

Rahab picked up a toddler and ran with all her might. The two men led the family toward the warriors advancing with their whoops and war cries. For a minute Rahab thought it was a trap and felt the child tighten his arms around her neck, but at the last second, they parted for them to pass through. The will to survive spurred them on until they reached the crowd of people standing at the edge of the river. After checking to see if everyone had made it, only then did she collapse to the ground in exhaustion as smoke from the burning city billowed in the sky.

Rahab and her family were allowed to live outside the Israelis camp. How she longed to actively worship the Lord God who had saved her and her family! She prayed to know how to become a part of His faithful people.

Solman often stopped to chat with Rahab when he brought supplies into her family. Her heart quickened every time she saw him, but she dared not hope for more. Then one day he motioned for her to join him in a place where they could be alone.

"Rahab, I have been given permission to propose marriage to you, and I hope you would be pleased to accept."

Surprise and delight overcame her, but still she felt compelled to remind him of her past life. "Surely you know I was only a harlot. I can imagine how much your people disapprove of who and what I am."

Solman's love for Rahab had grown strong, however, and he would not be dissuaded. "They also know how you saved our lives." Looking into her eyes, he said, "I know your desire to change and worship our God. It's sincere." He gave her a loving smile. "I believe you not only have found favor with Joshua, but our God. Joshua said an angel of the

Lord told him how to take the city. Maybe, my love, God sent us just to save you. He knew how much you wanted to serve Him." Drawing in his breath and putting his arm around her waist, he told her, "I have a high standing now and have been given one of the best parcels of property in the land, and we can have a good life."

"Not only has your God spared me, but He has given me a wonderful man and a respectable life!"

Thus, Rahab planned for the wedding she thought she would never have. She and her family were experts at making cloth out of the flax and working exquisite embroidery. When the day came, all the women admired her beautiful robe, though their admiration was mixed with disapproving stares.

It was not long before one of the Hebrew women ventured to ask, "Please show us how to make beautiful cloth and needlework like you do."

"Yes, I'll be glad to. I only have one request—that you tell me all about your God and how I can best worship Him," Rahab replied.

Once she began to teach the Israeli women the process of using the flax stalks to make cloth, they began to gravitate to her in spite of their initial shunning. She was able to meet a real need as God kept their clothes from wearing out until then and had guided them through the wilderness by a pillar of fire at night and a cloud by day.

Solman suggested, "Because of God's provision in the wilderness, we do not know how to raise crops, and I believe He saved your family to teach us how to grow food and till the ground."

Several happy months passed. One day as Rahab held her infant son, Boaz, her husband spoke to her with solemn pride. "The window of salvation came when you lowered us to freedom and allowed God's light to shine into your heart."

"Yes, our God has been good to us." Rahab smiled and bowed her head in gratitude to the God of Israel, whom she had come to know and love.

The story of Rahab can be found in these scriptures: Joshua 2, 6; Mathew 1:5; Hebrews 11:31; and James 2:25.

CHAPTER 4

Ruth's Loyal Reward

THE AROMA OF BREAD BAKING in an outdoor oven permeated the air as Ruth chatted with her mother-in-law and sister-in-law. Suddenly, they grew silent as they spotted soldiers riding toward them.

Ruth heard her mother-in-law's voice fill with anticipation as she said, "Maybe your husbands have returned from the war."

Before they could respond, the warriors rode into their midst, dismounted, and handed Naomi a scroll that brutally announced both of her sons had been killed in battle.

Ruth saw the other women's faces fall and turn to horrified grief that meshed with her own. While their tears fell, these ruthless men snatched loaves of bread and tossed them to one another like some kind of game. Then they helped themselves to drying dates and whatever else they could find before riding away.

As the reality of Ruth's loss began to sink in, she recalled how much she had loved Mahlon, this kind and gentle man who worshiped a God that did not demand human sacrifices like her people's cruel god, Chemosh.

Naomi spoke softly. "Without our husbands' help, we can't produce enough grain to pay for our property. In time, the three of us will be in serious trouble without food or protection. I've heard the famine is over in Israel, and home beckons me like a father with outstretched arms."

Ruth gave Naomi a startled look. "Are you telling us you want to go home?"

"Yes," Naomi admitted. "I'm thinking of returning to Israel."

"Then we're coming with you," Ruth replied. Orpah nodded in agreement.

So the next market day, they sold most of their valuables and made arrangements to leave. Daily they scanned the horizon for an approaching caravan.

"I see one coming," Ruth shouted.

"Hurry, put on your sandals and outer robes! Stuff your

deep robe pockets with fig cakes and dried meat and other supplies," Naomi said as they bound their skirts to make walking easier. "We'll put the heavier packs on our backs."

The caravan master folded his arms in front of his chest and shouted, "Pay up, or you'll not be allowed to go!"

"We must pay this exorbitant fee," Naomi whispered. "Although the master said it should only take a week, we'll have to travel at night and need protection from wild animals and bands of thieves. These men should know the best trails through the mountains and the safest places to cross the rivers."

Then Ruth noticed Orpah's tearful face.

Naomi shook her head. "This is not right. I can't expect you two to leave your homeland. Don't worry about me. I'll go back to Israel alone. You must stay and return to your families and find husbands."

Ruth looked on as Orpah made the heart-wrenching decision to stay in Moab, and they said their good-byes.

Then Ruth raised her head and looked straight into Naomi's eyes. "I'm going with you. Wherever you go, I'll go. Where you live, I'll live. Your people will be my people, and your God will be my God. Nothing but death will separate us."

Naomi was surprised at the elegance of Ruth's words and would not question her again.

After a difficult journey with Ruth supporting and

encouraging Naomi, the two women came to Bethlehem. Naomi remarked, "Will anyone know me?" She rubbed her forehead and sighed. "How much have things changed since I left?"

An older woman shaking rugs by her doorway stared at Naomi. "It can't be. After all this time, Naomi, is it you?"

"Yes, my friend, it's me, and this is my daughter-in-law, Ruth," Naomi said as the two older women embraced. Naomi's voice broke in stifled sobs. "Call me Mara, as the Lord has dealt harshly with me. My Elimelech and two sons have died, but Ruth has faithfully stayed by my side."

"Naomi, I'm so sorry. Come here and sit under my veranda, and I'll bring you something to eat," the older woman said as she gave Ruth a questioning look.

Soon word spread, and they were surrounded by Naomi's former neighbors and friends.

"You still have your land. However, after ten years, your dilapidated home is in need of much repair," one neighbor explained. "We'll supply you with materials and help you patch holes and repair the roof."

It was several days before the dwelling was fit to sleep in, but soon they had a humble place to call home. Ruth woke to the fragrance of flowering shrubs and warm April breezes.

She rubbed the sleep from her eyes. "We can't continue to live on the charity of your friends, Naomi. I noticed people gathering barley in a nearby field. If you agree, that's what I'll do," she said.

Naomi put her hand on Ruth's shoulder. "Bless you, my dear. By custom, you may gather whatever the reapers drop in the corners of the field."

The next day Ruth rose before sunrise and found a place to gather grain.

"Get out of the way, you heathen Moabite," one girl said as she bumped into her.

Ruth just stepped aside and kept gleaning. Just then a burly, dark-haired man grabbed Ruth around the waist, and she struggled to shove him away.

"Let the girl alone," an authoritative voice commanded. "Leave my property at once, and don't come back. That goes for anyone else who gives this young woman any trouble."

Ruth bowed low and looked up into a handsome, smiling face. He was somewhat older but was lean and well-groomed and wore a turban and robe made of fine cloth.

"Why have you shown mercy to me, a foreigner?" Ruth asked.

"My name is Boaz," he replied. "I've heard of your kindness to your mother-in-law, Naomi, and for this may Jehovah bless you. When the reapers break for lunch, come eat and drink with me from the fresh water the young men have drawn."

At lunchtime, Ruth followed the other workers. She sat in the shade and drank the water. Then Boaz came and joined them as the communal plate of dried corn, bread, and wine vinegar was shared.

Afterward, Ruth returned to the field and worked until dusk. When she went home, the grain had to be thrashed by beating it with a curved stick before she could go to bed.

Every day Ruth reported to Naomi all that had transpired. "I don't know why I've found such favor with Boaz as I'm a foreigner."

"I can guess. Boaz's mother was a Canaanite who was rescued from Jericho. Not only that, but she had been a prostitute. She was shunned for a while but showed our women how to make clothing and became a devout follower of Jehovah. She faithfully taught Boaz the ways of the Lord."

Naomi watched Ruth as she continued to tell her about Boaz. One day, Naomi asked her a surprising question. "Do you care for him enough to want him for a husband?"

Ruth's head came up, and her eyes widened. "What are you saying? I could never hope to marry someone of his position and wealth."

But Naomi continued. "Over the past few weeks, I've listened to you and watched the way your eyes light up when you talk about him. I think you're in love with him, and from what you've told me, I believe Boaz loves you too. Besides, he is obligated to marry you because of our Levitical marriage law. If he is the nearest relative, he must redeem our property and marry you to produce an heir."

"But Naomi, I don't want him to have to marry me," Ruth responded.

"He may not want that either. I have a plan that will decide the matter for both of you. Tonight Boaz will finish threshing and stay to guard the harvested grain. Go and wait until he has eaten and fallen asleep. Then, lie at his feet and at midnight uncover them to wake him," Naomi said.

"Naomi, this doesn't make any sense, but I trust you and will do as you ask." Ruth put on her best robe and dabbed on perfume from a precious vial she had brought from Moab. Then she made her way to the field and quietly crept to the hard, bare dirt threshing floor and lay down at Boaz's feet and listened to his gentle snoring.

She did not sleep as questions raced through her mind. *What if he rejects me and I never see him again?* Nevertheless, when the time was right, she uncovered his feet.

"Who goes there?" Boaz asked. His first thoughts were of someone stealing his newly harvested grain.

Ruth responded, "Don't be alarmed. It's your handmaiden, Ruth. Forgive me, but Naomi said you were a near kinsman. She asks for the redemption of her property, and if it pleases you, it would include me." In the moonlight, she could see him smile. The look in his eyes dispelled her doubts.

"How happy this would make me," he replied. "But there is another who is a closer relative. I must confront him first. This is a delicate matter and must be done right. The first thing tomorrow, I'll go see him. Now take a bushel of grain and leave before sunrise so no one sees you."

As she carried the barley home, she was overjoyed to know that Boaz shared her feelings. Still, she was afraid the other relative might claim her. What kind of life would she have then?

Boaz wasted no time in calling the elders together as witnesses to face the closer kinsman. Ruth and Naomi clung together and strained to hear what was being said. Boaz's servant motioned for them to come forward.

A man with disheveled hair and a dirty, tattered robe appeared. When he spoke, his mouth revealed a few remaining discolored teeth. "Yes, I've wanted the property for a long time."

Ruth's heart sank when she heard these words. However, Boaz was not about to let his newly found love slip by so easily. Boaz spoke up quickly. "You know when you buy the land, you also must marry Ruth, so as to give her dead husband an heir to the property."

This dissuaded the relative as he didn't want to lose any inheritance for the children he already had. "I've changed my mind," he said. "I lay aside my claim to it, and you are free to purchase it." He took off his sandal, which was how they measured the property, and handed it to Boaz to seal the deal.

Naomi turned to Ruth, vigorously hugging her. "This is the custom in our community, and now you are free to marry Boaz."

Soon a crowd gathered to congratulate Ruth and Boaz. Taking Ruth's hand, Boaz said, "I want you and Naomi to prepare for the wedding ceremony and feast tomorrow. I'll see to it that you have everything you need."

Early the next morning, Boaz's handmaidens came for Ruth and Naomi and took them to a room in his home. The maidens came laden with towels for bathing, perfume, robes, and jewelry.

The head maid told Ruth, "If this meets with your approval, Boaz would be honored if you would wear the wedding robe of his mother, Rahab. He was devoted to her and admired her faith in God."

Ruth was overjoyed! She had never seen any garment and veil so beautiful. It was embroidered with delicate grapes and leaves.

Ruth stood beside Boaz under the tallit shawl held up by poles at the corners. It had the family design that symbolized the wings of Boaz's protection. Ruth performed all the Hebrew traditions, just as Naomi had instructed.

After the festivities, Naomi turned to go back to her shack when Boaz came after her.

"Where do you think you're going? My home is large enough for you, too." Boaz gently put his arm around Naomi's shoulder. "You can get your things tomorrow."

The love between Ruth and Boaz grew, and in time they had a son. The whole community rejoiced, and the neighborhood women gave the baby the name of Obed, which means one who works/serves.

With Boaz standing next to her, Ruth handed her newborn to Naomi, who had suffered so much loss. She could see Naomi's eyes sparkle and her joy return. The promise of laughter and childish play would bind them all in family ties. Ruth said, "This child will inherit your property and take care of you in your old age."

Naomi pressed her lips to the child's forehead and looked up with eyes full of love. "You have given me a new family, and my life is complete."

Obed's grandson, David, became king and was in the lineage of Jesus Christ. This all happened because Ruth was loyal not only to Naomi but also to the Hebrew God, by whom she was truly blessed.

This story is found in the book of Ruth.

CHAPTER 5

Abigail Saves Her Household

"ABIGAIL, WAKE UP. YOUR BRIDEGROOM has come!" her mother's voice rang out. Abigail sat up and pushed back her dark hair. Tears began to slide down her lovely face. She had a sinking feeling in her stomach, knowing this would be her wedding day.

Her friends used to tell her she would probably get the best catch in all Carmel because of her beauty and intelligence. If only her father had not accepted a large dowry from an older man, and someone she barely knew. When she had protested, her mother pointed out he was a wealthy sheepherder and this was how things were done in Israel.

"Nothing can be changed now. Trust Jehovah to help you," her mother said as she dabbed at the salty moisture on her daughter's face.

The smell of meat turning on spits wafted through the air as Abigail walked over to the window. Outside servants scurried around cleaning, decorating, and preparing food. All too soon, it was time for her to put on her embroidered wedding robe and begin the ceremonies.

Abigail wondered if anyone could hear her heart pounding as she stood next to Nabal and they took their vows. She winced as she saw his protruding belly hanging over his belted robe. She looked up at his ample face and frowned at his graying beard and thinning hair.

What will my life be like? What kind of man is he?

When the wedding feast began, Abigail noticed a neighbor looking bored. It was because Nabal talked incessantly, bragging he had three thousand sheep and one thousand goats. Then after a servant splashed wine on the table, she heard Nabal burst out, "Watch out, you clumsy oaf."

What a terrible disposition, Abigail thought. Nabal was the one who had bumped the man's arm. Nabal by now had consumed several glasses of wine. Could this be the reason for his terrible behavior?

The first rays of sunlight streamed through the window, and Abigail slowly opened her eyes. The awful truth dawned on her. Her husband was bad mannered, self-centered, and unpleasant.

Not one to feel sorry for herself, she set about the task of organizing the household. As she observed the servants' abilities, she assigned them to cleaning, cooking, gardening, and other chores. The domestic help was grateful to work with this pleasant and reasonable young bride.

In the evenings, Abigail would listen to the servants discuss the latest happenings of Israel.

"Saul, king of Israel, has driven David, our national hero, from his home!" Jethro exclaimed as he stroked his graying beard. Jethro was Nabal's wise and capable overseer.

"Is he the one who was anointed by the prophet Samuel to be Israel's next king?" a maid asked.

"Yes, and King Saul is very jealous. Now it's rumored that David and his men are hiding out in a cave near Carmel," another servant stated.

"Have you actually seen this David?" Abigail asked.

"Many times he and his men have protected us and Nabal's herds from neighboring raiders. Please don't tell Nabal," the herdsman confided, "but because of his harsh manner, some of the men have joined David. I hear he has about six hundred men."

The next day Abigail looked up from her preparations

for the coming sheep-shearing holiday and saw Jethro running full speed toward the house.

Abigail went outside to meet him. "What's wrong?"

Jethro bowed and blurted out, "You have to do something to save us. Nabal has offended David's men and ultimately David himself. His men were here and asked for a portion of food for the protection they have provided. It's customary to set aside some bounty in appreciation. Many lawless and wild men would take over everything if not stopped. We have plenty for the holiday, but Nabal refused and even insulted them, calling them a worthless gang of roughnecks. When they left, their faces were crimson with anger. This could mean trouble for all of us—even our lives!"

Abigail shook her head. "Nabal won't listen, so there's no point in trying to reason with him. Quickly gather bread, wine, meat, grain, and fig cakes and pack them on donkeys."

When Jethro returned, he bowed and showed her what he and the rest of the servants had gathered. "We have two hundred loaves of bread, two large skins of wine, five dressed sheep, five measures of parched corn, one hundred clusters of raisins, and two hundred fig cakes."

"I see you have them all loaded on the donkeys ready to go." Abigail gave them an approving smile. "These should appease David's anger. Go on ahead, and I'll catch up with you," Abigail told Jethro. "Don't any of you tell Nabal where

I've gone." Silently she thanked the Lord the household was in order.

Abigail ran into the house, colliding with some of her maids standing inside the door listening. "Hurry! Help me get dressed to meet David. All our lives are at stake," she said.

A few minutes later, she stood before her handmaidens as they exclaimed, "You look as beautiful and regal as a queen! We pray you'll find favor in David's sight."

Abigail bid them good-bye and climbed upon a waiting donkey. As she urged the little beast along, Abigail wondered what she would say to David. Perhaps he would think she was too bold in coming. *I've heard he's a man after God's own heart. Maybe if I appeal to his faith in God and acknowledge the fact that he is anointed to be king of Israel, I can get him to listen to me.*

Her thoughts ended as she caught up with Jethro and the supplies that hung from the loaded animals. They watched as a cloud of dust appeared, kicked up by several hundred marching feet. A young man approached, leading men armed with spears and swords gleaming in the sun. Others had bows strapped to their backs. This had to be David. His hair hung to his shoulders with highlights of red as the sunlight and breezes teased it. He had a ruddy complexion and was muscular with finely chiseled features. She could see in his eyes a sense of purpose and noticed the respect his men gave him when he moved and spoke.

Abigail quickly dismounted and prostrated herself before him. David waved his men to a halt. With trembling hands, she brushed back a strand of hair. She had to be effective in her appeal for the sake of all her loyal servants. Looking up at David, she said, "I am Nabal's wife. Please listen to what I have to say."

David's brow furrowed, and his steel eyes bored through her. He crossed his arms and nodded for her to continue.

"I apologize for my husband's bad behavior. Let the blame be on me." Abigail shuddered at the idea that his men could just run a spear through her if he gave the order.

David's facial features softened, and he bent down and extended his hand to help her up. Did she imagine it, or was he reluctant to let go? With her hand by her side, she squared back her shoulders and stood straight.

"Did your lord send you?" he asked.

"No. I knew nothing of his refusal to give you supplies. He's a fool, as his name indicates." Abigail motioned to the braying donkeys protesting their burdens. "As you can see, I have furnished all the food you asked for and more. I appeal to your faith in God and your good judgment as future king of Israel to forgive my husband and spare my household."

Abigail continued her eloquent plea with carefully chosen words. "You fight the Lord's battles," she said, adding, "but the lives of your enemies He will hurl away as from the pocket of a sling." She watched his face and could see he was listening intently. "When the Lord has done all these good things for you, let this not be on your conscience, that this shall be no grief to you, nor offense of heart to my lord, either that you have shed blood causeless or that my lord has avenged himself."

The anger melted from David's face, and in its place was a look of admiration.

Abigail was spent and at the last she didn't know why she had said them, but these words slipped out: "Please remember me."

David replied, "God bless you for your good sense, for I swear by the Lord God of Israel that if you had not come to me, neither Nabal nor any of his men would have been alive tomorrow. Don't fear for your husband or your household."

"I am so grateful that you have shown us mercy." Abigail bowed again.

David smiled, extending his hand to help her climb on her ride. As their two hands touched, a look of hope passed between them even though both knew it could never be. When Abigail turned her donkey around to leave, David shouted after her, "Go in peace."

Jethro soon caught up with her. "Mistress, you were wonderful. You said just the right things." He gave her an admiring glance. "David's countenance turned from fury to respect, and he was awed by your beauty. You thoroughly persuaded him to change his plans and spare our lives. For this we will forever be grateful."

Tears formed in her eyes. "I couldn't bear to see anything happen to you and the others." Abigail flashed him a smile. "You servants have become like family to me."

As they approached the house, her thoughts of David's kindness were interrupted by sounds of boisterous celebrating. Nabal was roaring drunk!

What a fool, she thought. *Doesn't he know how close he came to losing his life! I'll deal with him tomorrow.*

The next day Abigail waited until Nabal woke up and was sober before she approached him.

"Where have you been?" he demanded. "You were not here to greet my guests!"

Bursting with contempt, Abigail replied, "Do you know what almost happened while you were celebrating? I had to appease David's wrath by pleading for our lives and offering him the food you refused. He was on his way to kill you and your men."

Nabal spewed out, "How dare you defy me behind my back."

His face contorted with indignation, and Abigail dodged a fist swung in her direction. Then Nabal clutched his chest and fell to the floor. In spite of all the care she gave him, after ten days, Nabal died. Abigail was shaken, but at the same time, she was free from this oppressive man. When the necessary funeral arrangements were made, she was surprised so few people came.

After the customary time of mourning, Abigail answered a knock at the door. A man bowed. "I am David's personal servant, and he sends his condolences upon the death of your husband. However, he does have a request."

Abigail, with her servant's heart, set about washing the messenger's feet. As she sponged water over a foot in the basin, she asked, "What food or supplies does he need?"

"He doesn't desire anything from your household— only you!"

"Me?" Abigail said in disbelief. "What do you mean?"

"Your haunting beauty has lingered in his mind, and he marveled at your wisdom and courage in coming to him." The messenger slipped his dried feet back into his sandals. "He was so impressed that he wants you to become his bride. Therefore, I am sent here by David to receive your answer."

Abigail smiled as she thought of David. What a wonderful feeling she experienced at the mention of his name! She could still see his sun-browned face and tender eyes with that look that was meant just for her. It was more than hope now. She knew David lived in continual fear for his life, yet she would leave her home and risk the dangers of hiding out to be with him. She reminded herself that she was David's third wife, and he now lived with one named Ahinoam, but this was the custom of the times. She continued to muse about how much better it would be to live in caves with someone she cared for than to have everything and be with someone she detested.

When Abigail looked up to reply, the man was intently looking at her and nervously twisting his hands.

"Tell David I'll come in a few days and bring five of my handmaidens with me," Abigail answered.

Relief flooded the man's face. "David will be so pleased. You will not regret your decision."

Finally Abigail's entourage and all their belongings were ready. As they approached, David came to meet her. His smiling eyes assured her of hope fulfilled. How different this wedding was! Just servants and David's men watched as they became husband and wife.

The next morning, Abigail awoke to hear water dripping somewhere in the cave and listened to the cheerful chirping of birds. She had forgotten how musical those lovely sounds were. What was this euphoric feeling? Then she remembered, *I am married to David.*

Abigail leaned over, ran her fingers through his hair, and softly whispered, "How very much I love you, my husband and future king of Israel."

This story can be found in 1 Samuel 25:1–42.

CHAPTER 6

A Queen with a Purpose

Part I—From a Peasant Girl to the Palace

THE TWO BEST FRIENDS LAUGHED in a carefree manner as they had come to view the gathering of many beautiful girls from all the 127 provinces. They walked past rows of vendors' tents with braying donkeys tethered behind. The front sides were rolled up to display wares such as tapestries, jewelry, and rugs. Stands with roasted figs, dates, and nuts enticed the crowd. In the center of the plaza, many lovely girls lined up to enter the palace.

A man with a large turban on his head announced, "If there are any more girls who wish to compete for the queen's crown, please step forward at this time and see if you are selected."

Hadassah knew the king had banished the former queen for not appearing before him when commanded, and now he was searching for her replacement.

"Hadassah, you could easily be selected," Tamar said. "You are by far the most beautiful girl here, and your cousin Mordecai has educated you well. Plus, everything you say and do seems right."

"No thanks," Hadassah replied as the girls eased their way into the crowd. "My cousin would never allow me to become a part of this. He's been like a father to me since my parents died and wants the best Jewish life for me. I will be betrothed next month to a boy who I'm excited about."

"Look, there is an opening." Tamar pointed. "Let's get a better view."

After they reached the front, Hadassah heard someone say, "Come here," and one of the men in charge had his eyes fixed on her.

She shook her head sideways. "But I don't wish to enter."

The overseer took her by the arm and pulled her into the center of the square. "You have no choice. The king has given me authority to select whom I wish."

His words were underscored by several soldiers standing next to him staring at her.

Each girl was dressed in her best robe, but Hadassah had only what she wore for cooking and cleaning. She was astounded that she had been taken out of the gathering.

Me, thought Hadassah. She could hear the crowd applauding, but all she could think of was, *I've got to clean the veranda and make supper.*

Just then Mordecai came running into the square. "You can't take her. We never agreed to send her to the palace."

"She's going now and has a short time to prepare for her trip." The eunuch crossed his arms and glared at Mordecai with steely eyes. "We're leaving soon," he said.

"I need a moment with her, and she has to return for her robes," Mordecai said.

"There's no time. She'll have plenty in the palace. You only have a few minutes together," the man said.

Hadassah and Mordecai hugged, and then Mordecai whispered in her ear, "Listen to me. You must never reveal your race. To conceal it, you will now call yourself *Esther*, meaning star. I'll try to get in touch with you. God be with you."

An attendant took Hadassah's hand and helped her into what looked like a lavish, small tent resting on poles borne by four men. Once the curtains were closed, tears trickled down her face. Then she sighed and thought, *Perhaps Mordecai can contact me since he works at the palace gate and this will soon be over and I'll be home again.*

Pulling back the folds in the fabric of the traveling tent, Hadassah could see the ornate gates as they passed through. What she saw was like entering into a make-believe world.

Beautiful gardens rested beside shimmering pools and fountains surrounded an immense palace with huge marble pillars. The people inside were lovely beyond what she thought possible. But there were guards everywhere.

"We have another contender from Susa," proclaimed the agent as her litter was lowered.

Hadassah was introduced to Hegai, the person in charge of all the girls. He was about Mordecai's age, with a graying beard and eyes that smiled. His robe was immaculate and as he came near, a wonderful scent wafted through the air. His presence was a relief compared to the gruff men who had brought her here.

"Welcome to the palace. What's your name, little one?" he asked.

"Ha ..." slipped from her lips, but then she caught herself. "My name is Esther."

"Come with me, and I'll show you where you'll stay," Hegai said.

Still in awe, Esther followed.

Here she was wearing everyday clothing without having had any time to properly fix her hair. She felt a twinge of insecurity as she moved through the palace and heard the girls giggling.

"Ignore them," Hegai advised. "You'll soon be as beautiful and more so."

Once all the contenders were gathered, Hegai instructed them on how to prepare to meet the king. Some girls were from prominent families and thought they knew more than him. They appeared to be about her age, with some younger or older than her sixteen years. Others were so excited they paid no attention to his long speech, but Esther hung on every word.

Esther was punctual for her beauty treatments, spent her spare time learning about the different provinces of the kingdom, and listened to Hegai as he explained the protocol of the palace. He gave her insightful nuggets of information about the king, which she stored away like treasure in a chest to delve into when needed.

A few days later while Esther was walking beside a pool, a girl named Jesreal said, "Well, I'm impressed with your progress. You're beautiful. What a remarkable change you've made."

"Thanks," Esther said. "Where are you from?"

"I'm the daughter of a governor from a distant province."

"You should stand a pretty good chance of becoming queen with that kind of background and your wonderful personality and beauty."

"Don't underestimate yourself. Hegai seems to have taken a liking to you."

Jesreal was right. Hegai soon picked Esther as his favorite. He even gave her a room of her own, with five servants to attend to her every desire.

Still the thoughts of home overwhelmed her, and as a maid rubbed perfumed oil into her skin, tears fell from her eyes.

"Mistress, why are you so sad? You have everything a young woman could want."

"I miss my cousin, who is like a father to me, and my friends," Esther said, choking back more sobs. "He works at the palace gate, but I'm only allowed to stay with the harem."

"I will check with one of the eunuchs and see if there is a place in the palace wall where you could talk to him."

In the evening while Esther was bathing in water scented in myrrh, Esther's maid exclaimed, "I have good news for you! Because you have found favor with Hegai, tomorrow you will be shown a place in a remote garden near the wall where you might talk to your cousin. It would be best not to tell anyone."

Esther dried herself off with a towel her maid handed her. "No, I won't tell. This would mean the world to me."

The next morning, her maid came in. "I'll help you dress, and then follow me."

Esther walked quickly through a beautifully trimmed

garden and a corner of the wall obstructed by bushes and flowers.

"Stay here and start singing a familiar song that your cousin will recognize and wait."

Esther sang a Jewish lullaby that Mordecai had taught her as a child. She went through all the verses over and over. Just when she was about to give up, she heard, "Hadassah? Esther, is that you?"

"Yes, how wonderful to hear your voice."

"I can't stay long, but how are you doing?"

"Oh, I miss you so much."

"You must stay positive and trust our God to help you. Keep a good attitude, and follow all the protocol that's required of you. The palace is a beautiful but dangerous place."

"Yes, I'm obeying and doing all that Hegai says. He has shown me favor." Esther traced the mortar in the bricks and sighed. "Will I be able to go home when this is over?"

"My precious one, you are now a permanent resident of the palace. We'll talk more. I must go now."

I'm now a permanent resident. Does that mean I can never leave? Esther mulled this over in her mind, and the truth slowly sank in. *I'll never marry my betrothed or go to the market with my friends.* She buried her head into her hands and let the tears flow. Then she lifted her head, wiped the moisture away, and determined to make the best of her situation.

A year had passed, and Hegai felt Esther was ready to meet the king. She had sought Hegai's advice on how to style her hair and what clothing and jewelry to wear. She was ushered into a room decorated in purple and gold, with lush carpets over marble tiles and tapestries on the walls. The flowing, tied-back drapes opened to a pool with a fountain surrounded by a garden.

She sat on a chair with a purple tufted seat. The arms and legs were overlaid in gold. She waited, knowing she was beautiful and dressed to perfection, but she also knew this alone would not gain the king's favor. Then she heard a swish and turned to see the king himself briskly walking toward her. She rose and prostrated herself in a bow. He was handsome and mechanically polite as he took her hand and led her through the drapes to chairs near the pool. She sensed he was preoccupied, and she was an intrusion on his thoughts.

Turning to her, he muttered, "There's a water problem with one of the provinces, though I don't want to bother you with it."

"I'm a good listener. I've heard that wells have dried up in certain areas. I've also read and seen the maps where the provinces next to them have mountains with many streams that would provide a good supply of water." *Oh why did I say that? I'm only supposed to answer when asked a question.*

With an astonished look, the king replied, "I'm surprised you know so much about it. My aides and I have spent much time discussing this." He continued to talk, knowing he had a knowledgeable listener.

A servant brought them their wine and a fruit tray with cheeses.

She took a piece of cheese and a few grapes when he offered her the tray and then proceeded to pluck several for himself. But in the process, the offending purple missiles flew up and bounced off her forehead. What a time for her to be amused. She tried to squelch a giggle, only to see him doing the same. They couldn't help but laugh out loud.

During the full-course dinner, Esther remembered Hegai's advice on how to properly eat and talk only when asked. Then they retreated to lounge near a fire in a metal pit, which cast a warm glow on their faces, reflective of the sparks igniting inside.

Then he ushered her into his private chambers. The king began to think on the many things he faced the next day and remarked, "After being with you, I can deal with anything tomorrow brings." He mumbled something she could barely hear. "In fact, with you I can face all my tomorrows."

After the evening was over, the king told her, "I don't

know why you are different from all the others, but I've fallen deeply in love with you."

The next day after Esther had returned to the harem, Jesreal exclaimed, "Hurry! We are all summoned to an assembly."

Esther quickly fell in behind her to hear the news and seated herself among the other girls.

Hegai rose to speak, and a hush fell as the girls stopped their chatter.

"I want to thank all of you for your participation in this quest for a queen, and I am pleased to announce the king has chosen a bride."

Sighs radiated around the room. Some had not even had a turn to meet the king.

"This high honor will bring with it much responsibility, privilege, and power. And now the lady's name you have been waiting to hear is ... Esther!" he shouted.

Looking around, Esther thought, *He can't mean me. There must be another Esther.*

Hegai stared right at her. "Yes, you. Congratulations! From now on you'll move into the queen's apartment and prepare for the royal wedding and your coronation."

Applause rang in her ears as she stood and followed Hegai to her new quarters. Her thoughts were jumbled in her head like hundreds of marbles let loose. *How does an orphan girl from a humble home who didn't even want the position become queen of a vast empire that stretches from India to Ethiopia? What does my God have in store for me?*

A huge wedding celebration that included everyone from the high officials down to servants took place. As Esther sat on the throne next to her king, he proclaimed, "Esther, I now declare you my queen as I place this crown upon your head."

Part II—Esther Risks Her Life for Her People

SOMETIME AFTER THE WEDDING, HATACH, Esther's personal servant, came running to her. "Your Majesty, I have a message for you from Mordecai and must speak with you privately."

"Come, we'll go into the sitting room in my apartment," she said. Once inside, she dismissed her maids. "Now you may speak."

"Mordecai has information for you to pass on to the king that two palace guards are plotting to assassinate him. You must tell him at once."

Esther was able to tell the king, and the would-be assassins were dealt with. She gave credit to Mordecai but did not reveal that he was related to her.

Esther knew that a man named Haman had recently been appointed prime minister with power next to the king. However, she received news that Mordecai refused to bow to him. Mordecai felt that one should only pay homage to God. This message was passed on to Esther, and she received reports that he was wearing sackcloth and ashes, which was a sign of mourning.

After Esther sent Hatach to Mordecai for further information, he returned with a worried look on his face.

"Come into my sitting room." Once they were in her

room out of anyone's hearing, she said, "Is there another plot against the king?"

"No, it's much worse!" The servant handed her a scroll.

Esther's face grew ashen as she read, "It is decreed that all Jewish men, women, and children must all be killed on the twenty-eighth day of February, and their property will be seized." With shaking hands, Esther handed it back.

Before she could speak, the servant implored Esther, "Mordecai says you must go before the king and plead for your people." Esther sighed, shaking her head. "He said to remind you that this has been posted throughout the empire."

Esther's voice betrayed her shock. "The king has not called for me for over a month. Everyone knows that if I go in without being summoned and the king does not extend his scepter to me, it would mean my death."

Hatach gave the message to Mordecai, and he quickly returned with a response. "Mordecai says that he believes God may have allowed you to become queen for such a time as this, and as a Jew, Your Highness, you and your family will not escape, either."

Esther knew the king had mood swings, and she never knew what state of mind he would be in. Shaking her head and gathering her courage, she replied, "Tell Mordecai to gather all the Jewish people and have them fast and pray for three days, and I and my servants will do the same. Even though it is forbidden, I will then go before the king, and if I perish, I perish!"

After three days, Esther stood in her room as her maids helped her put on her royal robes. She chose her perfume, hairstyle, and jewelry just as Hegai had advised her months before. Nevertheless, doubts and fears streaked across her mind like jagged flashes of lightning, but Esther knew she had to do the right thing and trust God.

"I'm ready!" Esther said as she took one last glance in the mirror.

Her entourage of maids accompanied her to the door of the inner court and bid her farewell and God's blessings.

Her heart pounded as her small hand grasped the massive handle to enter. She had to use her bodyweight to push the door open. Once she was inside, she could see the king, who was on his throne in the midst of a court procedure, stop in midsentence, staring at her in disbelief. All eyes were on Esther. As she walked forward, she wondered what he would do. His guards stood next to him with spears and swords that could end her life on the spot. Then she saw his face soften, and his arm reached out toward her with the scepter. She touched the tip, and relief rushed through her with such force it made her feel faint.

She reminded herself she must stand tall and continue her mission.

"What do you wish, Queen Esther?" the king asked. "I will give it to you, even if it's half the kingdom!"

Esther, realizing she not only had the king's favor but his generous offer to grant her whatever she wanted, said, "If it pleases Your Majesty and if you love me, I want you and Haman to come to a banquet I have prepared for you today."

"See to it that Haman comes to Esther's banquet, and tell him to hurry!" the king ordered his aides.

Haman arrived dressed in his finest, flipping his hair and smoothing out his robe as he sat down to dine. He talked incessantly about what the king and he had accomplished. He even made reference to a sect of people who were disrespectful to royalty and the kingdom.

During the wine course, the king again asked Esther what she wanted. Esther felt she needed more time and invited the king and Haman back the next night. What would the king think if he knew she was Jewish? Would he still be so generous with his offers of the kingdom?

Once more at the wine course of the second banquet, the king repeated his question. This time Esther knew she had to speak, "If it pleases Your Majesty, spare my life and those of my people."

She could see his face cloud up with anger as he asked, "Who would dare to bring harm to you?"

Esther stood to her feet and pointed to Haman. "This wicked man is our enemy!" Haman spewed wine from his mouth as his eyes widened with fear.

The king jumped up and went to the adjacent garden to contemplate what Haman had done and how he had been tricked into complying with it.

When he returned, Haman was draped across Esther, pleading for his life, which infuriated the king even more. The king roared with rage as he called the guards to take him away.

Because Mordecai had finally been honored just a few days before for saving the king's life, he was given Haman's job as prime minister. Following his appointment, Mordecai became more and more powerful. Haman's estate was given to Esther, and she awarded it to Mordecai. The king could not reverse what had been decreed, but he sent out another edict that permitted the Jews to gather and defend themselves on February 28, the day they were to be slaughtered. Under the old edict, the aggressors were allowed to take the property of the Jews, but when the Jews defeated their enemies, they did not take anyone's property. This day became a victorious celebration. It was remembered by a two-day festival called the Feast of Purim and commemorated each year, even to this day.

Because of God's great favor upon Esther, she saved her people. Though she had to risk everything to achieve God's purpose for her life, Esther became the most honored and powerful woman in her nation.

This story is found in the book of Esther.

CHAPTER 7

The Triumphant Journey

MARY RUBBED THE SLEEP FROM her luminous brown eyes, smoothing out her flowing dark hair. She put on the new linen robe her mother had made for her thirteenth birthday. This special day would be celebrated with family and friends.

As she entered the living section of her two-room home, her mother smiled at her as she prepared grain cakes for Mary's birthday.

Her father walked by and patted her on the head. "Don't

worry, little one. Now that you are of age, I'll find the best man in all of Nazareth."

"Father, I trust your decision."

Mary had been told she was a descendant of Rebekah, Rahab, Ruth, and Leah and eventually King David. These stories were told around the evening fires. However, she was far from actual royalty as her father struggled to pay the taxes and put food on the table.

She loved her small village of Nazareth that was situated on a hillside and enjoyed her neighbors. She remembered how she would bring food to those who were sick or went to help others until they were well.

At one such home, she had cooked and cleaned for two weeks while the mother was ill. She also recalled the older son, Joseph, who was in his early twenties. He worked with his father in the carpenter shop. He was tall and handsome and had the kindest eyes she had ever seen. One day he had arrived early for dinner, and she felt him watching her as she prepared the meal. In her haste to get everything cooked, she forgot the chicken on the spit over the open fire.

"I'm sorry about the meat, but I believe it still can be eaten," Mary said to the gathered family.

"That's okay. I like it a little charred," Joseph said as he brushed back a tuft of unruly dark hair. He had a twinkle in his eye, and she liked the way he smiled at her.

"Mary, stop daydreaming and hand me that dish," her mother said.

Mary shook the memory from her head and set about helping. That evening, the gathering sat under the goat-hair awning and ate their meal finishing with fig cakes. Mary's father stood and made an announcement.

"Mary, I have been talking to the family of our friends. We believe their son is one of the finest young men in Nazareth. He is working on his own home and is a good, honest man. Plus, his family is also in the lineage of David."

"Father, who is he?" she asked, sitting on the edge of her seat.

"We feel you will be pleased with him also," her mother added.

Her father looked directly at her. "Mary, Joseph is someone we trust to take good care of you."

"Is he the Joseph where I served?" Mary asked, not wanting to get her hopes up.

"Yes. He's the one. You must have made a good impression."

Mary couldn't suppress the smile that spread across her face.

"Mary, you look pleased," her mother said.

"I couldn't be happier."

That night Mary climbed the stairs to the little prayer

chamber on the roof. She knelt in prayer, thanking God her parents chose Joseph.

The following months went by in a blur, and Mary's family began to prepare for her betrothal. After this, it would be at least a year before she could expect Joseph to bring her into his house. Then a wedding celebration would follow. In the meantime, she was to remain pure.

Finally the day arrived as Mary stood with Joseph under the chuppah or canopy with just family and close friends. Joseph presented her father with the dowry coins, and he handed her a small wooden box with a finely crafted necklace of beads.

"With this, I pledge my love to you and declare you my wife," Joseph said.

"It's beautiful, and I will treasure it always."

They both sipped wine from the same cup, and a blessing was pronounced. Then the families celebrated, and she was betrothed.

Mary's days were busy preparing for her new home. But in the evenings, she ascended the steps to the roof of her prayer place, praying for her new life and the needs of others. It was here that a most unusual thing happened. Suddenly, a brilliant light appeared, and the figure of an angel stood before her. He had come from nowhere but looked as real as anyone she knew. At first she was afraid, and then the being spoke in a loving voice.

"Greetings," the angel said. "You are highly favored. The Lord is with you. Do not be afraid. You will be with child and give birth to a son and are to name him Jesus."

He continued to tell her more, and when he had finished, Mary asked, "How will this be as I am a virgin?"

"The Holy Spirit will come upon you and overshadow you," the angel said. "Even Elizabeth, your relative, is going to have a child in her old age, and she who was said to be barren is in her sixth month, for nothing is impossible with God."

Mary answered, "I am the Lord's servant. May it be to me as you have said."

Then the angel disappeared.

Mary knelt there for a long time, relishing the euphoric feeling of peace and joy. For several days she pondered this, telling no one.

"Mary, you seem so quiet, yet glowing with happiness. Is looking forward to your marriage the reason?"

"It's part of it, Mother, but a very special thing has happened. An angel appeared to me and told me I was to bear a child, and He will reign forever."

She heard her mother gasp, but she hurried to add, "Plus, Elizabeth will have a child also."

"Mary, you've always been so responsible and wise. You know your cousin is past childbearing age."

"Mother, send word to her by the next caravan. I was told she was in her sixth month. This will convince you."

So her mother sent the message, and Mary anxiously awaited the return of the caravan. When she spotted it in the distance, she and her mother ran to meet it.

"Mary, it is exactly as you said." Her mother now looked at her in shock. "Does this mean you too are expecting?"

"Yes, and I would like to return with the caravan to visit Elizabeth."

"I don't understand this! I never thought you would do anything to hurt Joseph and our family. If this is discovered, Joseph could refuse to marry you. You could be stoned to death!"

"Mother, I know this is confusing to you, but I have God's peace that He has chosen me."

Thus, Mary journeyed the distance to Elizabeth's home. When her cousin saw her coming, she said the babe leapt within her, and she knew of Mary's condition before she told her.

"What an honor that the mother of my Lord should visit me," Elizabeth proclaimed.

Mary fell into her arms, relieved that at last she had someone who understood and rejoiced with her.

Mary praised God that He had chosen her as a way to bless His people. She continued to rejoice and honor the Lord. Mary stayed three months to help Elizabeth with her pregnancy. Soon it was time to return home. She knew she would have to face the scorn of her neighbors and family, but the hardest of all was telling Joseph.

Mary waited in a garden to meet Joseph and could see him hurry in. Her heart soared to see him again, and she realized how she had missed him. He looked so happy to see her but stopped a short distance away, and she could see the hurt in his eyes.

"Mary, how could you do this to me? We had a wonderful life planned. I've worked all these months preparing a home and loved you so much. Now you've destroyed it all," Joseph said as tears welled up in his eyes, and he turned to leave.

"Joseph, wait! I've loved you too. Let me explain," Mary said

But Joseph spun around and ran.

Mary buried her head and sobbed. How could she explain? Would he turn her over to be stoned? No, she had to trust God. If He could do this miracle, He would see her through.

The following days were a mixture of knowing she was in God's plan, but her heart was full of sorrow, thinking she had lost the love and respect of Joseph. Later, she was surprised when Joseph asked her to meet him again in the garden.

"Mary, something wonderful took place last night," Joseph said. "God revealed to me that what happened to you is of the Holy Spirit. My heart rejoices once more. He told me the child should be named Jesus. I will come for you within the week."

But before Joseph came, it was decreed that a census would be taken. Joseph would have to return to his ancestral home. The wedding feast was cancelled as many others were also preoccupied with travel arrangements, so Joseph took Mary to his home. But she did not have long to enjoy it.

"Mary, I want you to stay here, where you will be comfortable and safe," Joseph said.

"No, don't leave me. It would be much easier for me to go than endure all the wagging tongues. I am heartier than you think."

"All right, we'll see if your parents will allow us to take their donkey."

As they left Mary's home, her mother said, "Mary, please be careful."

"Mother, God will help us on our journey. We'll soon be back and with the new baby in our arms."

But after all the other neighbors returned from the census, Mary and Joseph were not among them.

"Have you seen Mary and Joseph?" her parents asked.

One random traveler replied, "No, I believe the child was born, but they mysteriously disappeared. It was a good thing too. We heard Herod killed all the infants under two years of age."

Another added, "Many parents perished trying to save their children."

Mary's mother screamed, "No! Not my Mary and her family!" Then she collapsed, weeping.

In the meantime, Mary and Joseph's parents clung to the thin thread of hope, not knowing for sure what had happened. Then one day, down the dusty road of Nazareth came a young couple with their small son running and skipping.

"Come quickly," the neighbors shouted. "Could this be Mary and Joseph?"

Their parents dropped everything and ran to meet them, hugging and kissing the little family that was presumed lost.

Mary thought how good it was to be home and have the help and love of her mother again. After they were settled, the extended family came to celebrate their homecoming, bringing food for a feast. Mary was relieved that time had eased away the judgmental stares. Then after the meal, Mary and Joseph answered questions.

"Tell us why you didn't let us know where you were," Mary's father asked.

"We were afraid for our son," Joseph said. "After the wise men left, I was warned in a dream to flee to Egypt, and we stayed there until Herod died, and God spoke that it was time to come home."

"Did you have a comfortable place to deliver the baby?" Mary's mother asked.

"When we arrived, it was time for me to give birth, but every room in town was taken, so we were given a stable in a cave."

"Oh, how awful," Mary's mother exclaimed.

"It wasn't so bad. When the baby was born, we laid him in a manger. But you know something amazing happened that night. Shepherds were in their fields when they saw a brilliant light and a host of angels announced His birth. They came and worshipped Him, and God's presence was so glorious."

Joseph added, "Then after eight days, we took him to the temple to be dedicated, and a priest named Simeon approached us and asked to hold Jesus in his arms and announced, 'I have seen the promised one.' Then Anna, a prophetess, saw him too. She also declared the long-awaited Messiah had come."

The group sat in silence, and some shook their heads trying to comprehend what had been said.

"How did you survive when you went to Egypt?" asked Joseph's father.

"Three wise men from distant countries followed a star to our dwelling place. When they arrived, they presented Jesus with gold, frankincense, and myrrh. We used some of the gold to finance our escape until I could find work," Joseph said.

The evening lingered on until Jesus fell asleep on his grandmother's lap. As she brushed his hair from his forehead and kissed his cheek, she said, "Already he is wise beyond his years. I have watched him at play. He has won over his enemies with kindness and knelt beside a crippled child, comforting him, and had a calming effect on two boys who were arguing. He is young, but his wisdom and leadership are evident."

Mary answered, "Yes. We are truly blessed to be his parents. Joseph is teaching him his lineage, and we tell him of the stories of old." Then with a faraway look in her eyes, Mary lovingly looked upon her sleeping child. She remembered Simeon had said that a sword would pierce her heart, and Jesus would be rejected, but be the greatest joy of others. *What greatness is this little one destined to achieve? It has been promised that he will be a Savior, but at what cost?* Then she smiled. *For now, I'll love and cherish my little boy, our precious gift from God.*

Trials and triumphs come to us all. These young women had one common thread despite their various troubles and successes. It is a three-letter word—God. He has a plan for our lives, like Rahab, Ruth, and Esther discovered. They could not have dreamed what God had in store for them.

With God's help, may you overcome all your trials and achieve many triumphs.

CPSIA information can be obtained
at www.ICGtesting.com
Printed in the USA
LVOW11*1622280318
571475LV00010B/150/P